# IT'S RAINING BATS & FROGS

WRITTEN BY REBECCA COLBY

ILLUSTRATED BY STEVEN HENRY

FEIWEL AND FRIENDS

NEW YORK

A FEIWEL AND FRIENDS BOOK
An Imprint of Macmillan

Feiwel and Friends books may be purchased for business or promotional use.
For information on bulk purchases, please contact the Macmillan Corporate and
Premium Sales Department at (800) 221-7945 x5442
or by e-mail at specialmarkets@macmillan.com.

Library of Congress Cataloging-in-Publication Data Available

ISBN: 978-1-250-04992-6

Book design by Rich Deas

Feiwel and Friends logo designed by Filomena Tuosto

First Edition: 2015

10 9 8 7 6 5 4 3 2 1

mackids.com

For my parents, Myrna and Paul,
who never once rained on my parade

—R. C.


For Ladygirl,
'cause there's no nicer witch than you

—S. H.

Every year, Delia looked forward to flying
in the Witch Parade.
This year was no different, despite the
black clouds hovering overhead.

"I think it's going to rain," said Delia.

It did rain. Hard.
The witches were wet and miserable.

"It's raining on our parade," wailed one.
"Positively pouring buckets," moaned another.

That gave Delia an idea.

Delia whipped out her wand and began to chant:

It's raining, it's pouring,
but raindrops are BORING.
Change the rainfall on my head.
Make it CATS and DOGS instead!

The witches were thrilled . . . at first.

Then the parade came to an abrupt halt.

"This will never do," said Delia,
raising her wand a second time.

The raining and pouring
may have been quite boring,
but cats and dogs, they just don't work.
They hiss and bark and go BERSERK.
So, change what's falling on my head.
Make it HATS and CLOGS instead!

The witches were overjoyed . . . at first.

Then the parade erupted into a free-for-all.

Delia sighed.
"What a big to-do,"
she said, waving her wand again.

The raining and pouring
may have been quite boring,
but hats and clogs just have to go:
inciting fights, creating woe.
So, change what's falling on my head.
Make it BATS and FROGS instead!

The witches were ecstatic . . . at first.

But then the witches became even more wet
and miserable than before.
"What should we do now?" wondered Delia.

Delia had run out of ideas.

"Gnats and bogs?"
she mumbled to herself.

"Mats and logs? Rats and hogs?"

The more Delia thought about it,
the more she realized there was
only one thing to do.

With that, she raised her wand one last time and chanted:

The raining and pouring wasn't really boring.
And bats and frogs just make a mess.
They drop and plop and cause distress.
So, change what's falling on my head
back to drops of rain instead!

The witches were relieved. The parade soon proceeded.

And the longer it rained, the more exciting the parade became.

The floats began to float.

The marching band learned synchronized swimming.

And Delia and her friends tossed
water balloons into the crowd.

SCARECROWS UNION
123

Everyone agreed it was the best parade ever . . .

HAPPY HALLOWEE

. . . until the year it snowed.

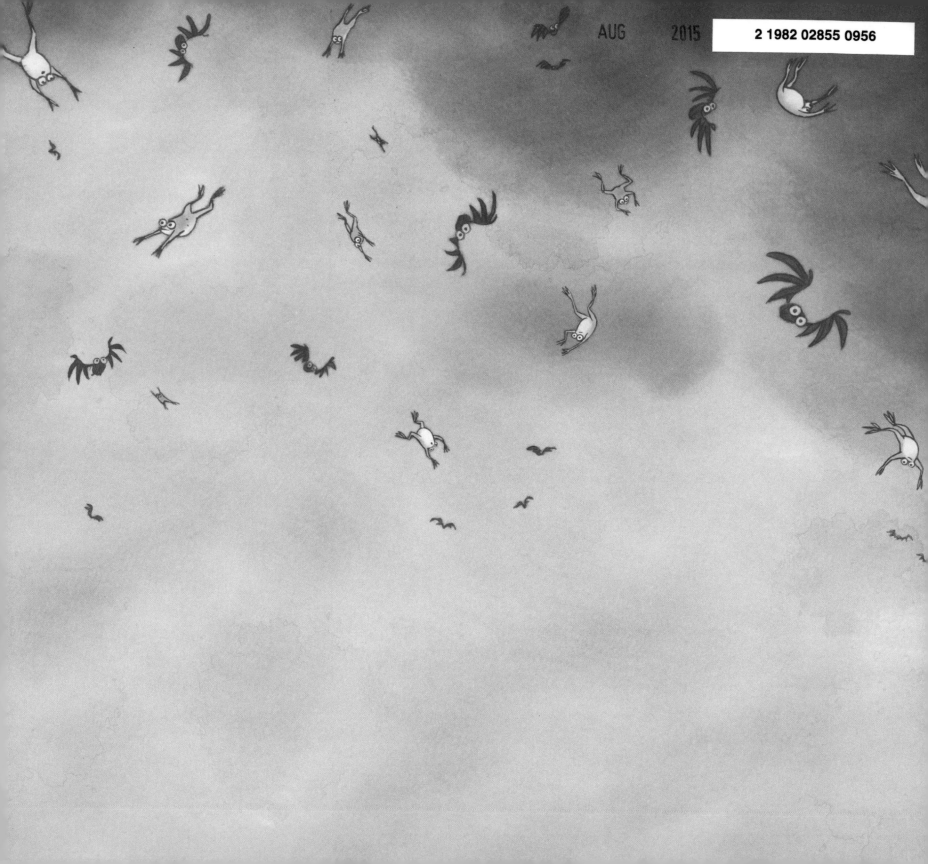